BLACK A

(A Whiskers, Wings and Bus
Comp

Terence Braverman

Other books in this series:

Whiskers and Wings (15 Tales of Countryside
Companions)
Autumn (A Time of Magic)
Links of Gold
Good Deeds and Evil Intentions

Other books for young readers:

Granddad Remembers (But is he telling the truth?)

Ninky and Nurdle (Tales from Noodle-Land)

Millie Manx (A Tale of a Tail)

Other titles:

A Twist in the Tale (A Collection of Short Stories)

The Man from Blue Anchor

Time To Kill

BLACK AS NIGHT

"It's not your brightest idea," said Percy Pigeon. He was perched on the long branch of the old oak tree outside Ollie Owl's home.

"In fact, it's one of your *darkest* ideas," he added.

Even Richard Robin found it hard not to laugh.

Ollie Owl scowled.

"Richard, my friend," he railed, "does something I have said amuse you?"

Richard Robin's face turned as red as the feathers on his chest.

"Certainly not!" he exclaimed, ignoring the smirk on Percy Pigeon's face.

"Nevertheless," he added, "is it a wise plan?"

"*Wise*?" Ollie spluttered. "Am I not the wisest owl in the whole world?"

"We've only *your* word for that," Percy replied.

"My dear friend," Ollie responded, "I have attended many academic establishments and been awarded numerous certificates."

"And I attended Poorly Pigeon Primary **and** The Sporting Academy for Racing Pigeons."

"Fat lot of good **that** did you," Ollie muttered.

"Pardon? Did you just speak? Did I just hear you remind us all of the year I won the British 300?"

"Twit!" Ollie said.

"Pardon?"

"I said to-wit-to-you."

"**STOP**! That's enough," Robin said. "Let's return to your idea, Ollie."

Ollie Owl harrumphed several times and carefully polished his spectacles.

Then he began.

*

Dotty Dormouse threw up her hands in horror.

 Normally of a very nervous disposition, she was now close to hysteria.

"I'm not playing his games," she said in a highly-pitched squeaky voice. "Ollie Owl can be very wise at times, as he is so fond of telling us, but this is foolhardy and senseless."

Dotty was sitting beside Mrs Woodmouse. Mrs Woodmouse ran the Fruit and Nut Shop in Undermead with the assistance of her son, Woolly.

"I'll make us both a nice cup of tea while it's quiet," Mrs Woodmouse said.

Dotty took out her handkerchief, blew her nose and took a deep breath.

"I can't let people see me in such a state," she said.

Mrs Woodmouse gave her a second handkerchief.

"This one is to wipe away the tears."

"But I'm not crying!" Dotty exclaimed.

"But I'm quite sure you *will* be," Mrs Woodmouse

4

responded.

The bell above the shop door jingled and Lord Hawley of Undermead entered. He removed his top-hat and inclined his head.

"Good morning, ladies," he said courteously.

"The usual?" Mrs Woodmouse asked.

"Indeed," Lord Hawley replied. "After all, I do believe it is *Friday*."

"I picked your order just before dawn. It's always freshest at that time."

"I'm as grateful as ever," Lord Hawley said.

Mrs Woodmouse took out a package wrapped in fresh leaves from beneath the counter.

"Six strawberries, ten blackberries and a handful of hazelnuts."

"Excellent!"

Lord Hawley turned to Dotty Dormouse.

"Now then, my dear, you're looking somewhat overwrought."

Dotty burst into tears.

*

Tommy Tortoise had raced three times around a buttercup growing in the front garden of The Big House. Then misfortune struck. It struck his nose. He clobbered it on a clothes peg that lay hidden beneath a tuft of grass.

"I was in training," he explained to Sammy Snail.

"With your eyes closed?" Sammy asked.

"Ollie Owl advised me to train with my eyes closed. He said I'd find it helpful."

"Ollie's a very wise owl, or so he keeps telling us all, but how exactly does hurling yourself around a buttercup with your eyes closed help?"

"It does sound a bit odd," Tommy admitted, "but he said it would prove useful in the long run."

"Don't talk to me about the long run," Sammy grumbled, "I'm having enough problems with a *short* run nowadays."

"Well, we do need to prepare properly," Tommy Tortoise said.

Sammy Snail sniffed the fresh air and considered his response. After a few minutes he shrugged his shell and said,

"Fancy a fresh dandelion for lunch?"

*

The bushy-tailed inhabitants muttered to each other as they stood and stared at the Undermead Notice Board.

"That's going to be tricky!" Squeaky Squirrel exclaimed. "Well, you can count *me* out," Cyril remarked. "I can still remember what *he* once told me."

'*He*' being Ollie Owl.

"Cyril," he said, "you are a diurnal creature which means you are not unlike Farmer Giles or Jack and

George from The Big House."

"But they don't have **bushy tails**," I said to Ollie, "and do you know what his answer was?"

"No idea," Squeaky Squirrel replied.

"He said…and I quote from memory…'*When I was at Owlbridge University, training to become the wisest owl in the whole world, I learnt about diurnal and crepuscular vision.*'

"Well, bless my soul, how interesting," Squeaky said and tried hard to suppress a yawn, "and what did he mean by that?"

"No idea," Cyril replied.

*

Roland Rabbit and Willy Weasel both stood panting beside the Undermead Notice Board.

"You put in a good finish," Willy said to Roland.

"And not a bad start, either," Roland pointed out.

"Ah, but just wait until tomorrow. Then you'll see

who's *really* the fastest creature on four legs in Undermead."

"So long as we play our game before nightfall," Roland responded.

Willy Weasel looked puzzled.

"Why is that?"

"Ollie Owl once told me I had crepuscular vision."

"Did he also tell you you've got a strange-looking tail?"

Roland Rabbit ignored the comment.

"Let's read the notice again," Willy suggested.

"We don't want to arrive too early."

"*You'd* probably arrive too *late* judging by your performance this morning," Roland retorted.

Roland and Willy played *Chase* almost every morning before breakfast but only *after* making their beds and washing up the previous night's dishes.

Their game of *Chase* followed a strange routine… Roland would stand on his back feet, toss his

"Yoo-hoo!"
yelled Roland Rabbit

head from side to side, poke out his tongue and waggle both of his front feet.

"Play time," he would giggle.

Willie Weasel always tried not to get annoyed…but then the taunts would begin…

"Willie Weasel's very feeble," or "Willie Weasel's looking evil,"

Willie would hurl himself forward, take three giant bounds and attempt to leap over the hedge that separated them. He usually failed, would end up crashing into the hedge and trap himself amongst its thorny branches.

Willie detested himself for it but had to admit that he enjoyed the chase that followed.

George was the young boy who lived at The Big House together with his younger brother Jack.

They both enjoyed tramping through the pastures and weaving between the trees that surrounded the vegetable fields of Farmer Giles. They felt perfectly safe because the animals and birds of Undermead kept a protective eye on them.

George had become quite adept at reading and pronouncing short words over the previous twelve months. Jack could make sounds, too, but their meaning was still a mystery.

"I will read this new piece of paper to you," George said as he and his brother stood in front of the Undermead Notice Board.

"Look, Jack. It's signed by Ollie Owl."

"Ooee," Jack said. "To-wittee-ooee"

"That's right! Well done, Jack."

George stood on tiptoe and began to read some of the words.

"To the in-hab-e-fants...the elephants...of Under-me."

Jack interrupted.

"Wooga-boogaloo."

"Whatever," George said and continued reading the words on the poster.

'F…fis is to in-form you all f…fat necks Sun-day we…weir all go-ing on a…"

"Dinner time, children. Hurry up or it'll get cold*."*

It was their mother calling to them over the fence that ran along the front garden of The Big House.

"Come on, Jack," George shouted. "We'd better hurry back!"

His words were carried on the wind, travelled along the winding lane, turned right on to the farm track and finally reached The Scarecrow.

"Clever lad, that," he thought.

"One day, he might write poems the equal of Percy Pigeon," and he repeated the rhyme he had just heard.

*'Come on, **Jack**, we'd better hurry **back**.'*

Of course, scarecrows are inanimate objects incapable of speech. Ollie Owl had declared it so…so it must be true.

*

Lord Hawley Housemouse had appointed himself spokesman for the residents of *The Home for Elderly and Retired Rodents.* As such, he regarded it his duty to make a statement.

He had summoned them to the Residents Lounge.

Harmony Housemouse had said that she would take the opportunity to sweep the floors, clean the cutlery and prepare lunch.

"Our dear wise and respected friend, Ollie Owl, has decided that we must all learn something new, especially those who prefer to snuggle into their favourite chairs at night and watch '*Wonder Mouse*' or '*The Rat who came in from the Cold*'.

Ollie continued,

"Indeed, we all need to enjoy new experiences, to seek fresh pastures…"

"And strawberries. We need to enjoy more strawberries," murmured Rickety Rat.

A buzz of approval ran around the Residents Lounge.

"Quite so," said Lord Hawley. "But what Ollie has in mind is…"

"And raspberries," voiced another elderly resident.

"Fresh carrots are worth a nibble or two!" exclaimed a carrot-loving rodent.

"And ice-cream!" said another.

Lord Hawley raised his walking stick, rapped it on the floor several times and frowned.

"*Attention!*"

The room fell silent.

"I will read you Ollie Owl's proposal. After that, we will vote with a show of tails and I shall then recommend a course of action. Those of you unable to raise their tail may twitch their whiskers instead. Twitch to the right for '*yes*' and twitch to the left for '*no*'.

You could have heard a pine needle drop as a hush filled the Residents Lounge.

'To the inhabitants of Undermead," Lord Hawley began, "this is to inform you all that next Sunday we're going on a walk…'

"A *what*?" shouted an elderly hedgehog holding tightly to his Whizzer frame.
"A walk, Oscar."
"A *walk?* Why do I want with one of those?"
Lord Hawley puffed out his chest and pulled himself up to his full height of ten centimetres.

"Questions later, Alfred. Now, if I could continue reading Ollie Owl's proposal."

'*Undermead can expect the appearance of a **phenomenon** before too long.*'

There was a high-pitched scream from Felicity Fieldmouse.

"I'm afraid of them noisy things," she wailed.

"No, my dear, you are **not**. It's the sound of a ***euphonium*** that frightens you."

"Oh, that's right. Sorry to interrupt."

'*The inhabitants of Undermead must be prepared and I, Ollie Owl, the wisest owl in the world…*"

"So he claims…" Hoppy Hamster chipped in, "but my Uncle Runaround says he once met an owl that could recite the alphabet backwards whilst standing on his head and knitting a cardigan."

Lord Hawley drew a deep breath.

"He must have found that exceptionally useful. Now…if I may continue…"

'…have come to a wise decision and it is my learned opinion that we, the inhabitants of Undermead, should meet this Sunday at fifteen hundred hours outside The Fruit and Nut Shop for the purpose of preparing ourselves for this forthcoming manifestation."

The elderly and retired rodents hadn't a clue what Ollie was talking about and even Lord Hawley was left baffled.

 At that moment, Percy Pigeon hurtled in through an open window and lay panting on top of Oscar's head.

"I know what's going to happen," he gasped.

"I found the answer in the book that Ollie lost."

"I didn't know Ollie had lost a book," Lord Hawley said.

"He…er… lost it just after I stole it!"

'A racing pigeon's eyes are as sharp as a hawk,
So I've nothing to fear from Ollie Owl's talk.
I bash into trees on the brightest of days so
I'm used to some bruises and head in a daze.'

Sadly, Percy Pigeon then clutched his head, murmured '*ouch*', keeled over, fell off Oscar's head and went to sleep.

*

Sunday arrived not long after Saturday and by two o'clock that afternoon Mrs Woodmouse and her son, Woolley, found themselves busy serving tea and freshly-made fruit scones to a large gathering of anxious Undermead inhabitants.

"Oh, dear, oh, dear," wailed Dotty Dormouse as she dabbed at the tears rolling along her whiskers. "I know I'm going to be terrified when I see it."

"Are you referring to *me*, by any chance?"

Dotty looked up into the big brown eyes of SwaggerWagger.

SwaggerWagger was the aristocratic Pekingese Chin Dog that, together with Curly Cat, looked after the family at The Big House.

"Oh, dear me, no!"

"Then perhaps you might be so brave as to articulate what it is that bothers you so?"

Dotty looked puzzled.

"Aunty Culate?" she asked, wiping her eyes.

"Ar-tic-u-late. It's an aristocratic word…just one of many that I learnt in the royal palace when I was growing up."

Dotty still looked puzzled.

"*Put into words*, Dotty. Or, as the uneducated Curly Cat might say, "*what's up?*"

Dotty Dormouse took a deep breath and then blurted out,

"The **phenomenon**. I'm afraid of the phenomenon!"

Ollie Owl was perched on the long branch that extended from his home in Old Oak Tree.

He looked closely at the shadow cast by the overhanging branch and made a calculation based upon information contained in '*Observation of the Sun and its importance in the calculation of Time – a guide for Wise Owls.*' and turned to page seventy-two.

He double-checked the formula:

$$171144cos(2.6491-0.0516083d)+0.381008cos(3.03481-0.0344047d)+23.258cos(2.97552-0.017203d)+0.377319$$

He figured it was two minutes to three and that the journey to The Fruit and Nut Shop would take one minutes and twenty-five seconds.

He adjusted the angle of the mortar-board on his head, checked he had his spectacles, and took to the air.

Another one minute and twenty-five seconds and he would disclose to the inhabitants of Undermead his wise plan regarding the phenomenon.

*

"Whiskers and wings and bushy tails of Undermead…you have, no doubt, been wondering what I've been doing over the past week."

"I hadn't noticed your absence," remarked Sammy Snail as he poked his head out from beneath his shell.

"*You* may have been unaware of my short sabbatical but *others* will have been concerned that I was not amongst them to offer my wisdom and resolve their problems."

"I can't say that I noticed either," Tommy Tortoise added.

"I *thought* it seemed quieter than usual," SwaggerWagger said.

"And we didn't lose any sleep worrying over another of your wise plans," Curly Cat pointed out.

Ollie swivelled his head three times to the right and once to the left, adjusted his spectacles and then spoke.

"Well, you're certainly going to lose some sleep *tomorrow*!" he exclaimed.

"Oh, *no*, oh *dear*, woe is me!" Dotty Dormouse cried out. "Don't worry, Dotty, I'll protect you," said Woolley Woodmouse.

"Protect her from *what* exactly?" Squeaky

Squirrel asked.

"From the…the…*thing*," Woolly replied.

"***Enough***!" Ollie Owl tu-whit-tu-whoo'd.

"I have been studying in great detail an addition to my library collection on the shelf labelled '*Academic Books for Wise and Perspicacious Owls*'."

"Here we go…" Percy Pigeon groaned as he turned to those beside him.

'*When Ollie Owl has a new book,*
  He puts on his glasses and dons a wise look.
  His remarkable wisdom is worthy of praise
  But sometimes his monologue goes on for days.'

"Very true," Richard Robin agreed, "but we shouldn't be too critical of him. Many a time one of Ollie's wise plans has saved Undermead from an unforeseen peril."

"That's very true," Ferdinand Fox said.

"Remember the great flood?"

Dotty Dormouse squealed.

"Please don't remind me," she wailed. "He climbed down the chimney to rescue me."

"And he saved our beautiful pastures from destruction," Ferdinand added.

"I think it was The Scarecrow did that," Percy pointed out, "together with Ebenezer Eagle."

"It was *all* of us! We *all* played a part in that," Richard Robin pointed out.

Squeaky Squirrel chipped in and said,

"But he *did* help my army of brave squirrels recover the nuts stolen by Bad Boy Badger and his Snooty Ooty Gang."

"*Silence, please*," Ollie demanded.

"*Quiet in the ranks*," Lord Hawley ordered.

Ollie Owl adjusted the angle of his spectacles and surveyed the assembled residents of Undermead. Then he began.

"I have been engrossed in the reading of a newly-acquired educational work on the universe," he began.

 "As a result, I have come to the exceptionally wise conclusion that we best prepare ourselves for what is to come."

In the silence that followed this statement one could have heard a feather drop.

"*Who made that noise*?" demanded Ollie and his left eye revolved twice to the right and once to the left.

"Sorry," said Percy Pigeon. "I accidentally dropped a feather."

"The calculations have occupied my mind and my time for several days. I have checked and double-checked and *triple*-checked and my conclusion remains the same."

Ollie Owl paused for dramatic effect.

"*But I have a plan…*a particularly *wise* plan, if I might be so bold, that will prepare us for what will shortly fall upon us."

With a soft sigh Dotty Dormouse fainted.

*

"We shouldn't have too much of a problem," Curly Cat said later.

"Although you'll have to watch that you don't snag that fluffy tail of yours on a bush." SwaggerWagger raised his aristocratic head and sniffed.

"I was taught to look after myself by no less a person than Minamota."

Curly Cat raised his more humble head and purred smugly.

"And *I* was taught by Buster O'Mulligan and they

don't come much tougher than that!"

"Ferdinand Fox shouldn't have much difficulty," SwaggerWagger said.

"And neither will Ollie Owl, of course," Curly Cat added.

"But I do worry for some of our little whiskered friends."

"Dotty Dormouse fainted, I hear." SwaggerWagger nodded.

"She'd faint at the sight of her own shadow."

Curly Cat purred in agreement.

"She's not likely to **catch sight** of her own shadow if Ollie's calculations are correct."

"That is most certainly true," SwaggerWagger said with aristocratic enunciation.

*

Ollie Owl could recall with clarity every single

word of the proclamation he had made in his address to the inhabitants of Undermead.

"I have completed my study of a recent addition to my collection of academic books."

"Is it *Percy Pigeon's Book of Pidgin-English Poetry?*" asked Ferdinand Fox.

Ollie Owl revolved *both* his eyes to the right three times.

"I am referring, too-wit-too-woo, to the learned work of a great Greek astrologer."

Ollie waited for another imbecilic interruption but, to his surprise, there was none.

"The book to which I refer bears the title '*The What, Where, When, Why, and How Guide to Watching Solar and Lunar Eclipses.*'

Dotty Dormouse had recovered her composure and asked,

*"**What, where, when, why, how……**?"* she squeaked, "can we start with the first question,

please, Ollie?"

"*What?*" Ollie asked somewhat caught by surprise.

"Thank you, Ollie. That's the one," Dotty replied.

"**What**."

"*What*? Ollie said once again after his head and eyes had stopped swivelling.

"*Yes*, I *just said*." Dotty Dormouse felt an attack of anxiety climbing her tail. "Followed by '*where*' *and 'when' and...*"

"Thank you, Miss Dormouse. I have captured the essence of your question."

Ollie had barely taken another breath when he was *again interrupted.*

"Please can you hurry things along a little," Henrietta Hedgehog pleaded.

Ollie Owl felt rage rise but before it could erupt from his beak...

"Only I've a strawberry pie baking in the oven."

The crowd cried "*Oooo*". *Everybody* enjoyed one

of Henrietta's delicious strawberry pies.

Ollie Owl ground his claws in frustration.

"***Very well***," he snapped. "I will elucidate."

Sammy Snail turned to Tommy Tortoise.

"What was that he just said?"

Tommy Tortoise tried to scratch his head but couldn't quite reach.

"He said he's going to hallucinate."

"Nothing new, then. Fancy a lettuce leaf sandwich?"

*

"As none of you will know," Ollie Owl began, "when the moon passes directly between the sun and Earth and its shadows fall upon the Earth's surface…"

"*I know*," somebody said.

Ollie Owl almost fell from his branch with shock.

"You can't *possibly* know," he said.

"Why not?"

"Because you're *Percy Pigeon.*"

"*Charming*," Percy remarked sarcastically. He fluttered up on to the shoulder of Woolly Woodmouse and focussed his attention on the inhabitants of Undermead.

"What our learned friend Ollie Owl will eventually get around to telling you is that we can expect the phase of a new moon shortly."

Ollie Owl hooted three times and spun round twice.

"Exactly! Just as I was about to say. Now…and this may take some time…I shall explain the consequences of such an occurrence."

Percy Pigeon piped up again.

"We can expect a solar eclipse," he said.

"A pair of *ear clips*?" Walter Woodpecker

muttered. "What am I supposed to do with **them**?"

Those who heard him burst out laughing.

"Switch on your hearing-aid," someone said.

Even Percy was speechless…but not for very long.

'When the moon finds itself caught 'tween the sun and the Earth

It gets ever so worried about its rebirth,

So it casts a great shadow on those down below,

Including old Ollie who'll claim that he'll knows

Of a very wise plan to deal with the dark

For all those left standing with their patriarch.'

"Percy Pigeon is correct," Ollie Own admitted.

"But I have a plan to help us through this darkest of nights that will soon be upon us."

To Ollie's astonishment an extraordinary event then occurred.

"Three cheers for Ollie Owl. He has a plan to save us all."

It was Richard Robin!

Richard flew between rabbits and mice; between foxes and squirrels and creatures that crawled; those that could fly and Percy Pigeon (who thought he could fly but was actually afraid of heights and was forever crashing into trees)…everyone, in fact.

Once the gathering had worn themselves hoarse with excitement, Ollie adjusted his spectacles again, corrected the angle of his mortar-board, and cleared his throat.

"Friends, country folk, inhabitants of Undermead, I come here today with a plan…not any old plan …but a wise plan to see us safely through a naturally-occurring phenomenon…"

"There…he's said it's again," Dotty Dormouse

cried out. "I don't like phenomenons…"

"Phenomen*a,"* interrupted SwaggerWagger. "The plural form."

"Clever clogs," muttered Curly Cat.

"I'm frightened of the plural form," Dotty moaned.

"It's all right, my dear," Mrs Woodmouse reassured her, "I'll not let them harm you."

"We must prepare ourselves for something none of us has ever seen before."

"If we've never, ever seen it how will we

recognise it? Will it say 'hello' or something?" asked Billy Badger.

"Twit-to-woo," sighed Ollie.

"Good question, Billy," Percy Pigeon said with a across his

beak.

"Answer his question, Ollie."

Ollie Owl rotated both eyes *at the same time* and in the *same direction*…which was quite a unique piece of visual acrobatics for him.

"I suggest Billy refers to '*The What, Where, When, Why, and How Guide to Watching Solar and Lunar Eclipses.*'"

"But you've got the only copy," Percy pointed out.

"Indeed. So I suggest you remain silent and listen to my exceptionally wise proposal."

*

"Of course, I spend most of my time living in a solar eclipse," Sammy Snail sighed.

"Ollie Owl hasn't told us precisely what it's like living in a solar eclipse," Tommy Tortoise said as he pushed the remains of a cabbage leaf towards Sammy.

"Dark!" Sammy said wistfully. "Very dark."

"Before divulging my wise but practical plan to you all I will use my extensive knowledge of both ornithology and our mischief of rodent friends…"

"Did I hear that correctly?" Harmony Housemouse asked indignantly.

Harmony Housemouse ran the Home for Elderly and Retired Rodents.

"He called my residents *mischief*!"

Ollie Owl paused in mid-sentence.

"It is the collective term for our mouse and rat friends," he explained.

"Well, please avoid using that collective term in their presence. Horace is easily upset and Mrs Matilda is quite unpredictable when she's angry." Ollie sighed.

The inhabitants of Undermead yawned.

"Get on with it, Ollie, there's a good fellow," Lord Hawley urged.

Ollie cleared his throat.

"Ferdinand and his friends will not be adversely affected as foxes have excellent night vision. However, our rodents are less fortunate but they have sensitive whiskers and that attribute *will* assist their navigation."

"How about *me*?" asked Roland Rabbit.

"Unfortunately, you have crepuscular vision so you don't see too well at night."

"And I suppose *you* can, being so clever and all?" Roland said.

"Alas, although I have binocular vision, my nocturnal sorties are occasionally brought to an abrupt end when my head makes contact with a tree."

"I know how *that* feels," Percy Pigeon called out.

"That's because your sense of direction and altitude is deficient," Ollie retorted.

Percy grinned, turned to his companions and said proudly,

"D'you hear that? It's not every day you catch Ollie paying me a compliment."

Olli rolled his eyes.

"Back to my plan…" he said.

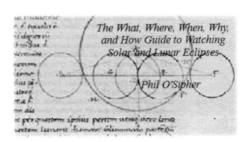

The What, Where, When, Why, and How Guide to Watching Solar and Lunar Eclipses

Phil O'Sipher

"Having read '*The What, Where, When, Why, and How Guide to Watching Solar and Lunar Eclipses*' and applying my advanced mathematical skills in order to create the relevant formulae…"

"Get to the point, O Wise One," Curly Cat called out, "or you'll feel *the point* of my claw on your…"

"Shush," Woolly Woodmouse whispered. "Ollie's doing his best and even *he* must be beginning to feel hungry."

"He could eat his words," Curly Cat snapped as he settled back down again. "He'd have quite a feast!"

"The conclusion I have reached, following the

aforesaid and having added my own calculations to the formulae, is that a solar eclipse will occur tomorrow at high noon."

*

A loud silence fell on the gathered inhabitants of Undermead.

It was broken only went Percy Pigeon asked another question.

"Do you mind if I check your calculations?"

"To-who-do-you think you are that you doubt the accuracy of accumulated academic knowledge?"

"Well, you see…as a former winner of the British 300…I had to figure out wind direction, wind speed, air temperature and produce a weather forecast for myself. I had to calculate take-off speed and angle of ascent as well as my rate and angle of decent in order to cross the finishing line with optimum benefit…and success, I might add."

Another silence was heard.

After several second Henrietta Hedgehog began to clap and she was quickly joined by her father, Happy Hedgehog.

Others then began to cheer and some even began singing.

"For he's a jolly good pigeon, for he's a jolly good pigeon…"

When everybody had run out of breath, Billy Badger asked, "What time *is* high noon?"

"High noon is what Humans take to mean twelve o'clock. It's not that precise but it suits their needs," Ollie explained.

"When is it high noon for our community?" enquired Henrietta Housemouse. "We use the traditional method," Ollie Owl replied and he turned to look directly at Richard Robin.

"*We*? Where do *I* fit into this all of a sudden?" Robin's feathers trembled anxiously.

Ollie adjusted his spectacles.

"After my early morning cup of Owl Brew Special Tea, I shall stand by the Old Oak Tree where you will measure the length of my shadow."

Richard looked stunned.

"*Why*, Ollie? Why?"

Ollie Owl smiled, a mysterious far-away look in his eyes.

"Percy. Perhaps you would like to explain to Richard how we calculate latitude and longitude." It was at this moment that Percy groaned loudly and fainted.

"Fortunately, I've already made those calculations myself. I've also measured my height without a hat," Ollie said.

"So you don't need me after all." Richard sighed with relief.

"*Au contraire*," Ollie replied demonstrating that he

knew two French words.

"I have prepared a shadow chart."

"*A shadow chart*," Richard echoed.

"Indeed. A shadow chart," Ollie said.

"Your shadow is longer at the beginning and at the end of a day. It's shortest toward the middle of the day…as noon approaches."

"I can't say I really understand but do continue," Richard sighed.

"I'm explaining this as simply as I can."

"Yes, Ollie. Thank you. Please continue."

Ollie continued.

"I've created a detailed chart. It's based on my calculations over each of the four seasons and shows the exact length of my shadow at any particular time of day."

Ollie Owl paused for three ticks of a cuckoo clock whist he allowed a hiccup to escape.

"Each time I shout '*now*' I will need you to measure the length of my shadow."

"I've never had need of a measuring stick," Richard Robin said.

"I would lend you mine but it's away being re-calibrated," Ollie explained.

Richard scratched his head.

"I could ask to borrow one from Matilda the Community Tailoress."

"Excellent!" Ollie declared. "I knew I could count on my dearest friend."

"Yes...well," Richard mumbled. "***Then*** what?"

"I will consult my Personal Shadow Chart and search its data for a shadow length that matches your longest reading."

"It sounds very complicated," Richard sighed.

"I'm explaining it in simple terms for the common beast and bird...robins excepted, of course."

Robin held his silence and kept his pride intact.

"I might let you borrow '*The What, Where, When, Why, and How Guide to Watching Solar and*

Lunar Eclipses.' It will explain how, in conjunction with my Personal Shadow Chart, I can forecast the date and time of a solar eclipse."

*

Ollie might have been right or he might have been wrong. He might have made it all up as he went along. Of course, he might actually believe it and it might actually be true. Only the Sun and the Moon and the Earth knew the true answer.

*

The inhabitants of Undermead were still gathered around the Old Oak Tree **and** they were still waiting to hear Ollie Owl's wise plan.
Some had fallen asleep; others were completing puzzles in '*The Undermead Gazette'*.
A group of young hedgehogs were singing '*Here we go round the Prickly Bush*' and even several frogs had journeyed from their pond at The Big House to play leap-frog.

Percy Pigeon chose this moment to wake up.

'Has Ollie announced what his plan is to be,
Or are we having to keep waiting to see?
I'm learning some somersault tricks in mid-air
And need to be sure that the ground will be there
When I land on my head, which I usually do,
And hear Ollie Owl say 'you-twit-too-woo.'

"Ah! Percy has decided to re-join us! Thank you, Percy," Ollie said.

"Have I missed anything important?" Percy asked.

Ollie Owl smirked.

"No…and *we* haven't missed anything important either."

Percy thought about this for three ticks of a cuckoo clock but found the effort very fatiguing.

Ollie cleared his throat in dramatic fashion, adjusted his glasses unnecessarily, and puffed out his chest importantly.

"I can now disclose my plan," he began.

"It is a plan that I am confident will see us safely through the phenomenon that will be thrust upon our doorsteps tomorrow at noon."

Dotty Dormouse raised a hand.

"Yes, Dotty. You have a question…*already*?"

"Should I move the milk bottles?"

Ollie was flustered.

"***Milk bottles?*** What the *Charles Dickens* do you mean?"

"I always put out my empty milk bottles on the doorstep ready for the milkmole to collect."

"That's very interesting, Dotty, but in what way is it relevant to my plan?"

"You said the *felomonomon* would land on my doorstep," Dotty wailed. She wrung her hands and turned to Mrs Woodmouse for consolation.

"It's all right, my dear," Mrs Woodmouse

reassured her and handed Dotty a dainty handkerchief.

"He was just being metaphorical."

Dotty began to wail all the more.

"Why does he have to be *metaformical* when he knows I'm frightened of long words?"

"I don't think he was ever aware of that," Mrs Woodmouse said with a frown on her face.

"*Nor was I*!" Dotty sniffed. "Until just now."

*

"The plan, the plan. We want to hear the plan."
The chant rose high into the air, swept around the Old Oak Tree, crept across pastures and settled amongst the bushes and thorns of Undermead.

"*What do we want? We want to hear the plan…*"

"*QUIET!*"

47

The inhabitants of Undermead were shocked into silence.

"I am Lord Hawley. You all know me. I organised the Battle for Undermead. We all came together as a community to defeat Bad Boy Badger and the Snooty Ooty Gang.

Ollie Owl says he has a wise plan. There *have* been times when his wise plans have left us questioning his sanity…"

"**Too-wit-too-woo…**be careful in your choice of words, your Lordship!" Ollie spluttered.

"…but there have been *other* times when he has demonstrated just how wise his plans can be."

"*That is so very, very true*," Ollie Owl said.

He adjusted the position of his mortar-board for no good reason other than effect.

"This evening…" he began again "when darkness descends and all is still within the wood…"

"And those throughout our neighbourhood

Are wondering what to do," 'Percy added.

"Ollie will too-wit-too-woo,

"And roll his eyes and stare at you."

Ollie glared at him.

"We'll practice things to do and say"

Percy paused for a tick...

"Until the danger goes away."

Roland Rabbit wrapped a scarf around Percy's head, tied it into a knot, and hauled Percy backwards and away from a scowling Ollie.

"This evening..." Ollie began again, "when darkness falls and all is still within the wood...we shall hold a practice drill."

Lord Hawley raised his umbrella to indicate he had a question to ask.

"And I'm putting Lord Hawley in command of the

49

operation."

Lord Hawley lowered his umbrella. His question had been answered.

"We shall gather here again at midnight. I suggest you each bring a candle."

"I have a pair of night binoculars," Lord Hawley said. "and a wooden rifle…although the handle's fallen off."

"And I have a rolling pin," Dottie Dormouse pointed out.

"My dear Dottie," Ollie said, "I'm not proposing we bake a cake!"

"Nor am I!" Dottie exclaimed.

"It's for protection."

"Protection against **what** exactly?" asked Lord Hawley.

"The *felongibong*!"

"The phenomenon won't hurt you, Dottie," Ollie said in a more kindly manner, "but **we** might accidentally hurt *each other* which is why I suggest we each bring a candle."

Ollie continued explaining his plan.

"Some of you have a degree of night-vision. Some of you have none. Some amongst you have sensitive whiskers and others smell."

"Steady on, old chap", said Bertie Badger. "Some of us can't help our smell."

"I'm referring to a *sense* of smell not the smell itself," Ollie replied.

*

"I would like you those of you with senses that work well in darkness to help those amongst you that are not as fortunate. I have chosen a few useful words. Please try to remember them."

Ollie cast one eye over the inhabitants of Undermead whilst, *at the same time*, he fixed his other eye on Percy Pigeon.

"And Percy…before you ask…*boo* is not

acceptable!"

"To warn others of your approach you should shout out the words *'flip- flop'*.
To warn others of a low overhanging branch use the words '*hang-bang'*.
To warn others of holes in the ground repeat the words '*mole-hole.'*"

Lord Hawley took over. "Men of Undermead. Look out for the ladies. They have a weaker constitution and are more easily frightened by an unseen enemy."
"Watch it, your lordship, or you'll feel my weaker constitutional whack you on

your head," Henrietta Hedgehog snapped.
"My apologies. How about *meeker* constitution?"
"How about I…"
There was a sudden kerfuffle and the crowded

parted to form a corridor down which SwaggerWagger strutted forward imperiously. Having reached the front of the gathering he turned and spoke.

His luxuriant tail and majestic head were raised as his aristocratic gaze swept slowly from left to right.

"My tutors at the palace taught me many things before our family was driven from home and country by the Uprising.

One thing I was taught to respect was *leadership*. This is what I suggest in order to bring our meeting to a close."

He sniffed the air.

"We will form several separate groups for tonight's practice walk. We will **all** learn Ollie's useful words and we will **all** accept Lord Hawley as our Commander-in-Chief."

A single hand-clap was soon followed by another.

A single cheer was quickly followed by two more. Within ten ticks of a cuckoo clock the countryside around the Old Oak Tree was filled with optimism and hope as the inhabitants of Undermead returned to their homes and prepared for the practice walk at midnight.

*

Not every inhabitant of Undermead was waiting at the Old Oak Tree as the hour of midnight approached. Two, in particular, made slower progress.

Tommy Tortoise had offered Sammy Snail a lift to speed up their journey. Sammy did not answer immediately.

"When we held our race last year neither of us beat the other," Sammy pointed out. "We finished together."

"In somewhat suspicious circumstances," Tommy said.

They winked at each other's little secret.

"Do you want a lift or not?" Tommy asked.

Sammy thought of the long journey ahead. Along a garden path, past the lettuce patch, turn left at the washing-line post and then follow the worn track to the Old Oak Tree.

It would exhaust him!

"Yes, please, I would appreciate a lift."

Tommy Tortoise lowered his head and Sammy crawled up on to Tommy's back.

"We're supposed to be there at midnight," he murmured.

Tommy Tortoise grinned.

"Ah, but Ollie Owl didn't say *which* midnight!"

*

Dottie Dormouse arrived. She was hanging on to

Mrs Woodmouse with one hand and holding her rolling pin with the other.

"I'm not taking any chances. You never know who might be lurking in the darkness behind a tree."

"This is simply a practice run," Mrs Woodmouse reminded her.

"Yes…and I fully intend to."

Mrs Woodmouse looked puzzled.

"Fully intend to do **what?**" she asked.

"Practice running!"

*

Richard Robin and Percy Pigeon sat chatting beside the tree and watched the excitement growing around them.

"What do you think Ollie and His Lordship have in mind?" Percy asked.

"Whatever SwaggerWagger **tells** them to have in mind, I guess," Richard replied.

Percy suddenly flapped his wings, flew into the air and promptly fell to the ground.

"What *are* you doing?" Richard asked.

"I had an unforeseen urge to practice an aerial somersault," Percy Pigeon replied rubbing his head.

Richard shook his head and smiled.

"Stick to poetry," he said. "It's safer."

"Why can't we all just stay indoors. That would be safer. Do we really need a midnight walk?"

Richard Robin shrugged his feathers and came to a very difficult decision.

"Do you promise not to mention what I'm about to tell you to anybody else?"

"Of course," Percy Pigeon replied. "You know me."

"Exactly!" Richard sighed and Percy grinned.

"Okay," Percy said, "…on this occasion you can trust me. Your secret will be safely stored in my wings."

Richard took a deep breath.

"There is something that Ollie forgot to do."

Percy stopped grinning. He frowned.

"This sounds serious."

"It is," Richard Robin said.

"When Ollie did his calculations he worked out the precise time that the solar eclipse would occur."

"I know," Percy said.

"But what you *don't* know is that Ollie forgot to calculate *how long it would last*. It might last *forever!*"

*

Lord Hawley had agreed to SwaggerWagger's suggestion and organised the inhabitants of Undermead into three groups. Each group had a leader and each leader carried an emergency candle.

SwaggerWagger would lead one group and

Richard Robin another. Mrs Woodmouse had agreed to her son, Woolley, leading a third. Ollie Owl, who was experienced in night travel, would fly overhead and oversee the operation.

It was a well-kept secret that Ollie was afraid of heights. Richard Robin knew. If trees had eyes they would know, too, of course, as Ollie often entangled himself in their branches.

The route Ollie had chosen would take the groups away from the Old Oak Tree and deep into the Forest of Undermead. Within the Forest there were three paths. Each group would take a separate path. Each path was loop-shaped so where you started was also where you finished. It was impossible to get lost.

The three groups would each begin walking, or stumbling, or flying around their allotted loop. The loops crossed each other in the centre of the forest at the signpost for Hawthorn Lane.

It would be the middle of the night. It would be dark. It would be like…an eclipse of the sun.

One group might bump into another.

There were roots that one could trip on.

There were rabbit holes into which a mouse might fall.

Lord Hawley blew a whistle and a hush fell upon the gathering.

"I shall shortly blow three short pips on my whistle. It will signal the start of our nocturnal adventure. Before I do, however, I would remind you of your duty to warn others of the perils they might encounter when it turns dark as night. Remember those cautionary words… *'Flip-flop, hang-bang and mole-hole'*

*

Lord Hawley sounded three short pips on his whistle.

SwaggerWagger swished his luxuriant tail, held high his aristocratic head and moved his noble feet forward at a genteel pace.

"Follow, please," he said in a refined voice.

Curly Cat asked, "Any chance of hitching a lift on your back, please?"

SwaggerWagger gave him a look that answered the question and retorted, "Listen up, keep up, shut ...!"

Richard Robin set off with *his* group.

Percy Pigeon was close behind and encouraged the stragglers to keep up by entertaining them.

"If you find you're left behind you might live to regret it.

There may be danger up ahead and please do not forget it.
You know the words you need to learn to warn of any danger,
If Dotty Dormouse turns to run then please try to restrain her"

Woolley Woodmouse felt quite important as he led his party to the start of *its* loop. His bravery was acknowledged by all following his courageous confrontation with Bad Boy Badger and the Snooty Ooty Gang the previous year.

Now, he made himself as tall as he could, walked with a confidence he didn't feel and smiled between teeth that were chattering.

Ollie Owl was overhead keeping both his eyes on everybody. He swivelled them right and he swivelled them left and sometimes he swivelled them both at the same time *but in opposite directions.*

Curly Cat coughed politely. SwaggerWagger pretended not to hear.

Curly Cat coughed more loudly and SwaggerWagger stopped and turned around.

"Yes?" he snapped.

"I thought we were heading towards Hawthorn Lane," Curly Cat remarked.

"Correct. We'll reach it quite soon," SwaggerWagger replied.

Curly Cat smiled smugly.

"I do believe you're going the wrong way,"

SwaggerWagger sniffed and looked down his aristocratic nose.

"We cannot possibly be going the wrong way," he said. "We are following a path that forms a loop. We follow the loop. We cannot get lost."

Although they were best friends, Curly couldn't resist grinning.

"We can if you're following the loop in the wrong direction."

There was a silence that lasted at least four ticks of a cuckoo clock.

SwaggerWagger brought the silence to a close by lifting his luxurious tail and swiping it across his head in frustration.

"*You're right*!"

"Actually…I'm right but you're *left*," Curly Cat replied. "We should have turned right when we set out. You turned left."

"If you knew…why didn't you say?"

"I tried but you pretended not to hear."

"Hmm…I apologise. In fact, I apologise twice. I'm in breach of my code of conduct and I have betrayed my royal ancestors."

Curly Cat had rarely heard SwaggerWagger apologise *once* let alone *twice*.

"May I propose that, having gone some way already, we continue in the wrong direction?"

Curly Cat suggested.

SwaggerWagger didn't want to embarrass himself further.

"Agreed!" he said, "…but we'll need to be careful not to bump into anybody coming towards us. Others may have gone wrong, too."

*

Ollie Owl picked himself up and shook his head to clear away the stars that were spinning around his head.

He had been keeping an eye on everybody from the air and now there was nobody to keep an eye on. Afraid to lose sight of them he had flown higher than was sensible for him and cleared the tops of trees – some of them quite tall.

Ollie was afraid of heights and began to have a panic attack. He'd felt dizzy. He'd felt himself falling…falling…falling… and as his head introduced itself to a tree trunk he had felt a moment's pain. His last thought was that he hoped nobody had lost their way.

*

Richard Robin continued to be entertained by Undermead's British 300 Champion and runner-up in the British Prose and Poetry Competition for Pigeons (or something like that).

'Although we know which way to go
It's easy to get lost,
It's dark and gloomy 'neath the trees
So keep your fingers crossed.'

Richard Robin wondered where Ollie Owl had got to. He was supposed to be watching and helping to guide them safely through the black night and the forest. Trees would suddenly spring up as if from nowhere.

He looked up and groaned.

At head-height-for-birds was a sign-post headed '***Bird Ramblers Walkway***'.

Below the heading it read, '***Route Three to Bramblebush Lane***'.

Bramblebush Lane? So where had he gone wrong? Where was ***Hawthorn*** Lane?

He was leading them in the wrong way direction!

*

Woolly Woodmouse was humming to himself. His group had encountered no problems and he reckoned they were almost halfway around their loop at the point where the three paths crossed. There had been no mishaps.

Everyone had avoided tripping over somebody else.

Nobody had been whacked by an overhead branch.

There had been no damaged bones, wings or whiskers as a result of unseen holes in the forest floor.

It was all going very well indeed.

There was an excited cheer as Woolly announced, "We're about to reach Hawthorn Lane. No accidents or injuries reported."

It looked to Woolly that his was the first group to have reached the signpost.

The three leaders had agreed to leave a small bundle of asparagus sticks at the Hawthorn Lane signpost, each tied with its own distinctive ribbon, to indicate that their group had passed through the crossroads.

The Community Seamstress had prepared three sets of ribbons.

One was red, another blue,
and the third was green.
Woolly lit his emergency
candle by rubbing two
twigs together and peered into the small pool of
light created by the flickering flame.

He could see no other sticks lying beside the
signpost. There were no sticks tied with a red
ribbon and no sticks tied with a blue ribbon.

He smiled contentedly and placed his own group's
sticks by the signpost. They were held together by
an elegant green ribbon.

*

"Has anybody seen Dotty Dormouse?" Mrs
Woodmouse asked.

"She definitely set out with us," said Ferdinand
Fox. "I *know* she did because she hitched a lift on
my back not long ago."

69

"Oh, dear! I should have taken greater care of her," Mrs Woodmouse groaned.

"Why? Is there a problem?"

"Yes, there most certainly *is* a problem! The only thing on your back right now is red fur."

"Cripes! I hope she hadn't fallen asleep."

"I'm hoping she hadn't fallen *anywhere*!" Mrs Woodmouse squealed.

"If she *had* fallen asleep on my back," Ferdinand Fox continued, "she won't have heard me shout '*hang-bang*' when we passed that ash tree with a low-hanging branch."

Mrs Woodmouse looked horrified.

"*Robin*!" she cried out. "*Stop! You have to stop!*" Richard Robin turned round. He looked concerned.

"Mrs Woodmouse? Is that you? Is something the matter?"

"Yes, it's me and, yes, something *is* the matter. We've lost Dotty Dormouse!"

"*Dotty! Can you hear me*?" Richard called out.

He'd told the rest of the group to remain with Mrs Woodmouse while he retraced the route they had taken.

He flew close to the ground calling out Dotty's name.

"***Dotty! Can you hear me? Where are you?***"

He thought he heard a tiny squeak.

"Dotty? Is that you?"

"Yes, it's me," the tiny squeak replied.

"Where are you?"

"I don't ***know*** where I am! It's very dark in here."

"Yes, Dotty. I understand…but where is here?"

"I don't know but I think I can see the branch of an ash tree above my head," she answered.

"Hold on," Richard Robin said.

"I've nothing to hold on to," Dotty Dormouse replied before adding, "I'm so frightened I think I might faint."

Richard found a small branch that he was able to lift and carry to the ash tree.

"Can you describe where are you, please, Dotty?"

"It's dark, it's deep, it's...*dreadful*!"

"I'm sure it is. Keep talking and I'll be guided by your squeaks."

Squeak, squeak, squeak.

Squeak, squeak.

Squeak.

"I've found a mole-hole," Richard Robin said. "Are you inside it?"

"I think so. I'm definitely not *outside* it!"

"I'm lowering a branch into the hole. Can you see it?"

"No...but I can *feel* it. You just bonked me on the head!"

"Sorry. Climb up the branch if you can."

"Of *course* I can. I'm not some helpless little mouse, you know," Dotty said indignantly.

Richard Robin sighed deeply. It was going to be one of those nights.

*

SwaggerWagger stopped abruptly and Curly Cat tripped over his lustrous tail.

"Take some care…*Cat*!" he snapped.

Before Curly Cat had time to think of an appropriate riposte Roland Rabbit had barged into her.

"Sorry," he mumbled. "Didn't know you were there. Did you shout *foot-fall*?"

"*Me*?" Curly said. "*You're* supposed to warn *me* of your approach."

"That's a bit difficult when I can't *see* you," Roland countered.

"Huh! This silly word business is not going to work. In fact…"

"*Ouch!* Who just pulled my ear?"

"*Ear*? I thought it was a piece of rag hanging off on a bush."

"*My ear?* A piece of *rag?*"

"It's terribly dark, you know," Roland replied, "and I needed a handkerchief because I'm about to…*achoo*!"

*

"How we are doing?" asked Sammy Snail.

"I think we're almost there," Tommy Tortoise replied.

"I hope we're not late," Sammy added. "I wouldn't want to miss the briefing."

"Don't worry. We've plenty of time," Tommy said.

"Enough time for a lettuce sandwich, do you think?" Sammy asked.

"Oh, yes. And plenty of time for a nap, too," Tommy Tortoise responded.

*

SwaggerWagger and Curly Cat thought they had completed almost half their loop of the midnight-walk practice.

The pace had been slow as SwaggerWagger had felt the need to wash his feet and the tip of his tail each time he spotted a dark stream meandering close to their path.

"Keeping one's extremities clean is very important," SwaggerWagger had explained. "Good hygiene leads to good looks."

"You should try it more often then," Curly Cat smirked.

SwaggerWagger ignored the comment.

"We would have made even better progress had it not been for my initial…er…mishap regarding the *faulty* signpost…"

Curly Cat shook his head and guffawed.

"The *signpost* was fine…the *signpost* knew where

it was supposed to be going…the **signpost**…"

SwaggerWagger's warning growl was both refined and aristocratic.

"*I take your point*! Maybe this could remain a little secret between the two of us?"

"Well…" and Curly Cat pretended to ponder the question.

"I have some chocolate-flavoured *Sniffy-Snacks* in my conservatory back at The Big House," SwaggerWagger remarked.

Curly Cat smiled wickedly.

"Signpost? What signpost? I've forgotten about it already," he said.

*

"*TOOT! TOOT!*"

"What's that?" Mrs Woodmouse looked at Dotty Dormouse.

"It sounds a bit like '*toot-toot*," Dotty replied. "It's

one of those cautionary warnings that Ollie told us about."

"Can you remember what it means?"

"Yes, Mrs Woodmouse, I can. It means someone is approaching…and I'm not even a bit mouse-squeak afraid!"

Mrs Woodmouse looked startled.

"The next thing you'll be saying is…"

"*Leave this to me,*" Dottie said firmly.

"*Halt*! *Who goes there*?"

"Woolly Woodmouse," Woolly replied.

"He claims to be your son, Woolly."

"Oh, for Goodness' sake, Dotty! Hello, Woolly."

"Hello mum. Is Robin here?"

Richard Robin hopped forward.

"Good to see you. We're just waiting for SwaggerWagger's group to arrive."

"They'll be fine, I'm sure," Woolly said.

"SwaggerWagger is a Japanese Chin dog with up-market training in tracking and trailing."

"I hope you're right," Richard Robin replied.

There was a silence but it was broken after only two ticks of a cuckoo clock.

Woolly looked concerned.

"But has anyone spotted *Ollie Owl*? He's supposed to be overhead keeping his revolving eyes on us all."

"Now you mention it, I have to say that I haven't spotted him for some time," Richard said.

It was then that Dotty Dormouse did something that nobody had ever witnessed before.

She made a sort of a joke.

"Ollie…if you can see us say *hoot, hoot.*"

The sky was very high up and Dotty was very low down.

There was silence.

*

Ollie Owl rubbed his head. It felt sore.

His eyes had stopped revolving but were only

half-focussed.

"Where am I?" he wondered, "and why am I here?"

He rose shakily to his feet.

"Who am I?" he asked himself, "and where was I going?"

He fluttered his wings and rose a few centimetres from the ground.

"*I can fly!*" he said in astonishment. "I've always wanted to do that."

He took several steps along a path beside him and asked himself another question.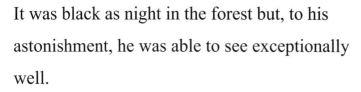

"I wonder if I have a home somewhere?"

It was black as night in the forest but, to his astonishment, he was able to see exceptionally well.

"Too-woo-too-wit," he said. "I can almost see as well as an owl."

*

SwaggerWagger's group had reached the centre of the forest and stood or sat or fluttered around the signpost for Hawthorn Lane.

Richard Robin's group was there, too, and it chatted or joked and generally pretended it was not afraid of the dark.

Woolly Woodmouse moved amongst the group and did his best to maintain their morale.

Percy Pigeon kept them entertained.

"We're waiting now for Ollie Owl
To say that's it okay
For us to form our groups again
And continue on our way."

Woolly Woodmouse lit his emergency candle as a guiding beacon for Ollie in case he couldn't spot them amongst the murky gloom cast by the trees.

Where **was** Ollie Owl?

*

Ollie Owl felt strange. He sensed that he should *be* somewhere.

He cast his eyes to a night sky full of twinkling stars.

He flapped his wings and rose a few centimetres into the vast space above him.

If only he could remember how to levitate higher.

It must be a wonderful feeling to fly, to have clouds floating above and trees swaying below, to feel the wind on his feathers and to look down on the world beneath him.

*

Percy Pigeon was growing impatient.

"If we're to practice walking back in darkness we shouldn't be hanging about. It'll begin to get light soon."

SwaggerWagger reluctantly agreed.

"We need to know he's safe, though. Something might have happened to him."

"Something certainly *has* happened to him," Percy retorted. "He's not here. *That's* what's happened!"

"I've an idea," Richard Robin said, "but it requires a pair of wings, a good sense of direction and the ability to fly at great speed "

SwaggerWagger looked thoughtful.

"Can't think of anyone that fits that description," he said.

"Er…" said a voice. "Excuse me."

"There's Penelope Peacock but she doesn't really know her north from her south."

"Er…excuse me."

"Or Fleetwood Jack, the Undermead long-hop champion," Richard Robin suggested.

"Er…excuse me."

"How about Postman Pat?" SwaggerWagger asked.

"You made *that* one up!" laughed Richard.

"Oi! You two! How about Percy Pigeon, the former British 300 Champion?"

SwaggerWagger and Richard Robin exchanged looks.

"Now, *there's* an idea…" said SwaggerWagger thoughtfully.

"*I'm on my way*!" Percy shouted as he sought a make-shift runway and prepared for lift-off.

"But you don't know where you're going," Richard pointed out.

Percy paused for a tick of a cuckoo clock.

"*I will when I get there*!" he blurted out and, with a yell of '*chocks-away*,' sprinted along the path and ascended into the night sky.

Moments later, there was a soft thud as Percy Pigeon hit the ground, somersaulted twice, and landed in a bush close to Richard Robin.

"Ouch! I should have asked…where am I going?"

*

Ollie Owl was puzzled. He felt as though he *ought* to know many things. He *ought* to know where he lived and he *ought* to know where he was.

He had a pair of wings. He *ought* to know how to use them. He *ought* to have an ability to fly.

He looked up once again at the night sky and admired the twinkling stars and a full moon. Tomorrow, the stars and the full moon would most likely make way for blue skies and sunshine.

Something seemed to suggest to him that daytime was his natural time for sleep and that he was only *truly* awake at night…just like an owl.

He sighed. He could never be an owl. Owls were very wise. Some owls were *so* wise they could read and write. Why, the wisest owl in the whole world was probably able to read a scientific publication such as…

'The What, Where, When, Why, and How Guide to Watching Solar and Lunar Eclipses'…

…which was the moment that his left eye revolved twice, his right eye revolved ***three*** times and he could see clearly without his spectacles.

*

"Are you quite sure you know which way you're heading?" Richard Robin asked.

Percy Pigeon looked slightly offended.

"I can only go in one direction," he quipped.

Richard knew there was more to come. He wasn't disappointed.

"Which direction is that?" he asked.

"Depends which way my head's facing. I just follow it. Sometimes it's difficult to keep up."

"We need to find Ollie Owl," Richard said. "He might be in trouble."

"But I'm about to race to the rescue!" Percy declared. "Did you not know that I'm a former British 300 Champion?"

"You tell us all at least twenty times a day."

"*Twenty*? That's very clever of you…being able to count up to twenty. How many *is* twenty? I suppose it's because you spend so much time in Ollie's company."

Richard frowned.

"I'd like to spend a lot *more* time in his company but that won't be possible *unless you find him!*"

"Say no more! I'm on my way!" and Percy rose rapidly from the ground and shot off in the wrong direction.

"*THE OTHER WAY*," Robin shouted.

Percy spun around in mid-air, turned a somersault, dipped a wing in   acknowledgement and set off in search of Ollie Owl.

Ollie Owl studied the stars and used his knowledge of astronomy to determine 'north'.

He opened his owl pack and withdrew a map of Undermead. The signpost for Hawthorn Lane, which stood in the centre of Undermead Woods, was marked with red berry juice. He decided to make that his starting point and if nobody was there he would make another decision and he would keep making other decisions until he'd decided what to do.

He fluttered his wings and raised himself a few centimetres from the ground.

Ollie repeated this eleven times, hopping higher each time as his confidence grew.

"I *can* fly! I *can* fly!" It was like a mantra!

He repeated it to himself eleven times and then sprang from the ground. With a triumphant hoot, he rose as high as his fear of heights allowed.

At about the same time, Percy Pigeon headed away from the signpost at the centre Of Undermead Woods and those gathered around it, and went in search of Ollie Owl. He couldn't resist a parting rhyme.

*

"I'm on my way to Ollie, the sky's as dark as black,
And then, when I have found him, we'll both be flying back.

If Ollie is the wisest owl the world has ever seen
He'll pretend he wasn't lost at all and question where we've been.
He'll say the routes we've taken are not the routes as planned.
That he'd explained them clearly so we all could understand.
He'll say he chose his wisest plan to guide us

through the night

To simulate conditions when tomorrow's has no
light.

To prepare ourselves for darkness as we face the
sun's eclipse,

Now raise three cheers to Percy for his
entertaining quips!"

"Good luck, Percy!" those below called out.
"Return safely with Ollie Owl!"

*

Ollie Owl felt confident he was taking the fastest
route to the crossroads and the signpost to
Hawthorn Lane. It took thirteen wing-flaps before
he realised that his fear of heights had
disappeared…at least, for the time being!
He sailed above trees without crashing into their
branches. He swept across meadows without a
single mid-air collision. Regrettably, unused to

such vigorous exercise, he ran out of fuel and was forced to land.

He landed beside an ant-hill.

His tummy rumbled and he took out a piece of Henrietta Hedgehog's blackberry pie from his owl-pack.

"*Oi*! Watch where you drop your crumbs!"

Ollie Owl sat stock still, the pie hanging from his beak.

"Somebody has to sweep up after you!"

Ollie turned his head to one side, looked down, and was startled to see a fierce-looking ant waving a broom at him.

"Who are *you*?" Ollie asked.

"Angus Ant. *Mister* Angus Ant to you. No respect for the countryside, some people!"

"Do you *have* many visitors dropping crumbs?" Ollie enquired.

"More than you might imagine," Angus Ant

replied.

"Rabbits are the worst," he continued.

"*Rabbits*? *Really*? Ollie asked. "I'm very well-read but that is a fact I have not discovered in my extensive research into such matters."

Angus Ant giggled.

"Ah, well, you see...rabbits are always leaving *their litter* behind!" and Angus scuttled away chuckling to himself.

It never failed.

*

Percy Pigeon swept from the darkness of the wood into the darkness of the night sky.

Percy and Ollie shared one thing in common. Both were afraid of heights...with one important difference.

Ollie Owl may have been known for his wisdom but he certainly wasn't noted for his speed. If *he* hit a tree it was usually *gently* and painless.

Percy Pigeon, a former British 300 Champion,

hit a tree, it would be fortunate to remain undamaged.

"I **mustn't** be afraid…I **must** be alert," he kept telling himself as he dipped and dived and wriggled and weaved between trees.

"Ollie? Can you hear me?"

*

Ollie Owl sighed, closed his owl-pack, and took flight again.

He took pleasure in listening to all the nocturnal echoes that bounced around him.

Night-time was definitely the best time of the day.

 From all directions came the warbling and screeching of both residents and tourists. He heard crickets and grasshoppers in the meadow below and a nightingale sang from its perch upon the bough of a tree.

Ollie acknowledged several '*too-wits*' and '*too-woos*' as they reverberated through the woods…

…and then he heard a voice that broke the magic spell.

"*Ollie? Can you hear me?*"

The voice grew stronger as it drew nearer.

"*Percy Pigeon racing to your rescue!*"

Ollie Owl faced a predicament.

Should he call out to Percy or let him fly past?

"*Ollie. I need to find you!*"

In a hushed voice, Percy added,

"To be honest, I'm hoping you might rescue *me*. I'm completely lost!"

Ollie Owl sighed deeply.

"Come over here, you foolish pigeon. I'm on the branch of a beech tree enjoying my final moments of tranquillity."

A few wing-flutters later and Percy was perched

beside him.

"I bet you're glad to see me," he said. "I've come to save you!"

"From what, exactly, am I being saved?"

"From being lost, of course! I've been hand-picked to rescue you and return you safe and sound to Undermead."

"What the Charles Dickens are you talking about, you silly p…"

"Poet?" Percy suggested.

Ollie's eyes revolved three times in each direction.

"*I'm not lost*," he roared. "*You are*!"

"I thought so," Percy grinned and then he asked a question.

"Ollie…you're knowledge and wisdom surpasses all understanding."

"That is generally accepted as being so," Ollie replied.

"Well, tell me this, O wise one…"

Ollie twitched his eyebrows.

"I hope this is not going to be another of your silly questions."

Percy solemnly shook his head.

"If I flew upside down would I arrive back where I started?"

*

"Percy Pigeon has been gone a long while," Curly Cat remarked.

"Where do you think he is?"

SwaggerWagger lifted his nose and sniffed haughtily.

"Lost! That's where I think he is."

He was proved wrong because at that moment the sound of squawking and angry words filled the air. Two ticks of a cuckoo clock later, a bundle of feathers landed on the ground. The bundle of feathers contained Ollie Owl and Percy.

"Mid-air collision," Percy explained.

Ollie's eyes revolved at such speed he had difficulty stopping them.

"If you hadn't attempted a somersault around the branch of that tree there would not have ***been*** a collision," he said.

"True," Percy admitted. "So how is everybody?"

Richard Robin hopped forward.

"First of all – thank you for rescuing Ollie."

Ollie opened his beak to protest but fortunately no words escaped because Robin gave him a warning glance.

"Next, to answer your question, everybody who set out walking at midnight managed to reach the signpost to Hawthorn Lane safely."

SwaggerWagger considered mentioning Dotty Dormouse's mishap but thought better of it.

"Er…hmm," Ollie interrupted.

"I believe the intended course of action was that

we each completed our circuit…not give up halfway round."

Woolly Woodmouse stepped forward.

"We had to make a decision. You weren't here so *I* had to make the decision for you."

"Er…hmm…very wise of you."

A gleam appeared in Ollie's eyes.

"This is why I deliberately delayed my return."

"Why would you do that?" Woolly asked.

"To test your leadership qualities, of course," Ollie Owl replied, "and you passed! I will inform Lord Hawley of your success."

*

SwaggerWagger, Richard Robin and Woolly Woodmouse sat by the signpost and listened as Ollie Owl outlined his *new* wise plan.

"It is not long now until the break of dawn," he explained.

Nobody was surprised. They could see for

themselves that the sky was growing lighter as the sun crept above the horizon.

"While there is still time…before we are again drowned in darkness…"

Ollie Owl paused for dramatic effect but nobody noticed.

"What *I* think we should do," SwaggerWagger butted in to say, "is that we use whatever daylight is still available and all head back together as one group."

"You took the very words straight out of my beak," Ollie blustered.

"And return to our homes," added Woolly Woodmouse.

"Well, yes, of course. That's part of my new exceptionally wise plan," said the wisest owl in the whole world.

"And prepare ourselves for the *lips of the sun*," added Percy Pigeon.

There was sudden, complete silence as everybody stared open-mouthed at Percy and the broad beam on his face.

"I was only pretending I didn't know the word
To describe what is coming to each beast and
bird;
But Tommy the Tortoise and Sammy the Snail
Have a special eclipse that sits on their back
And whenever they wish their daytime turns
black."

Percy waited patiently but there was no applause so he walked away nonchalantly and whistled a tune to himself as he went.

*

The journey back to the heart of Undermead was

faster and less eventful for everyone than the one that had taken them out to the crossroads and the signpost to Hawthorn Lane.

Dotty Dormouse took out her broom and swept some leaves from her doorstep. She went back indoors to the drawer marked '*Cleaning materials*' and took out the brass polish and a duster. The candlestick would need to gleam brightly before the eclipse arrived because, when it ***did*** arrive, she wouldn't be able to find it unless it was glowing in the dark. Dotty glanced at her cuckoo clock.
There might be time enough for a second cup of tea.

*

"Do you think this is the right spot?" Sammy Snail asked.

"My eyesight's not so good without spectacles," Tommy Tortoise replied, "and I forgot to bring them."

"There's a feather or two lying around and one of them belongs to Ollie Owl," Sammy said.

"My Goodness, Sammy. How do you know that?

"There's some writing on it. It says, '*if found, please return to Ollie Owl and receive a lettuce leaf as a re*ward.'"

Silly Snail, Tommy thought.

"Well, I feel quite certain we've arrived at the correct place even if nobody else has arrived yet," he said.

"I warned you we should have slowed down a bit!" Sammy chided.

"And it appears you were right," Tommy Tortoise said.

"Anyway, no worries. I don't suppose they'll be long. Shall I unpack the lettuce sandwiches?"

"Good idea," Sammy replied. "Followed by a long

nap."

*

The sun was rising higher as the Whiskers, Wings and Bushy Tails of Undermead wound their way home.

Ebenezer Eagle had now joined Ollie Owl, Percy Pigeon and Richard Robin. They kept two wing-spans apart from each other to avoid accidents and Percy had been warned against performing somersaults.

They glanced down at the motley group beneath them. Everyone appeared to be in good spirits and morale was high.

Dotty Dormouse had put on a wide-brimmed hat as protection from the sun and Curly Cat was trying very hard to provoke SwaggerWagger.

"When we set out at midnight you were leading our group. Where did you think you were taking us? The back of beyond, that's where."

SwaggerWagger ignored him.

"***Best foot forward,*** you ordered. What happened to *your* best foot then?"

SwaggerWagger took a deep breath.

"Back at the palace, where I grew up, we were taught to be polite," he said.

"Back at the Centre for Abandoned Cats, where *I* grew up, we were taught to respect our betters."

"Your point being…?" SwaggerWagger asked.

"If you're one of the ***betters*** how bad are the rest?"

SwaggerWagger turned to face Curly Cat.

They stared at each other for several ticks of a cuckoo clock and then suddenly burst out laughing.

"It's my turn now…" SwaggerWagger said.

It passed the time.

*

The sun in the clear blue sky was close to reaching its zenith.

Roland Rabbit was sitting comfortable in his cosy home reading the most recent copy of *The Underground News*. His close neighbour, Ferdinand Fox, would probably be doing much the same.

They lived either side of The Scarecrow which Ollie described as an inanimate object incapable of speech. For an inanimate object incapable of speech it had managed to scare Ollie a time or two…but not in this particular story.

Cuckoo clocks were ticking away the time until Undermead turned black as night.

Dotty Dormouse felt there was just sufficient time to have a final cup of tea. The polished brass candlestick was on a table close by. She would light the candle at the very last moment. The wick might need to stay alight for a very long time. She checked the window was firmly closed. It *might* help keep out the solar eclipse.

Squeaky Squirrel had invited two of his chums to snuggle down beside him inside his home. He lived in an oak tree but it was neither as grand or as old as Ollie Owl's but then it didn't need to be. Squeaky Squirrel had no need for shelves to store the piles of books and scientific equipment that Ollie found so essential. So long as he had a bowl of nuts to hand, he and his chums could survive the mysterious phenomenon which was about to descend upon them.

*

Ollie Owl took a book from one of his shelves. The shelf was labelled *'Books for Owls Educated to Higher Tree Degree Level'*. The book he took from the shelf was the one he had been studying for several months and upon which all his calculations had been based.

The title of the book was…

'Observation of the Sun and its importance in the calculation of Time – a guide for Wise Owls'

He would pass the final moments before the solar eclipse by marvelling at the scientific formula he had translated into Owlish.

He hummed quietly to himself as he perused the

numbers, double-checked his use of brackets and reminded himself of the importance of '*ΔT*' in his calculations…*which is when he began to tremble uncontrollably.*

He had discovered an error in his arithmetic!

ΔT=62.92+0.32217*t+0.005589*t2

ΔT=62.92+0.32217*t+0.005589*t2

Where:

y=year+(month−0.5)/12

y=year+(month−0.5)/12

t=y−2000

He had written down the number at the beginning of his calculation incorrectly! He'd written:

ΔT=62.29+0.32217. He **should** *have written:*

ΔT=62.92+0.32217.

*

Ollie Owl sharpened a pine needle and secured his hastily-written note to the front door to his home in the Old Oak Tree.

He then went back inside and bolted the door top and bottom.

The note read:

'No deliveries today! No visitors! I'm not at home!'

*

A strange silence had fallen over Undermead. The leaves hanging from the summer branches of trees were trembling, as if anticipating a sudden gust of wind might blow them away at any moment.

Percy Pigeon and Richard Robin sat on cushions on the counter of The Fruit and Nut Shop. Mrs Woodmouse, who owned the shop, stood behind them. Woolly Woodmouse was humming softly to himself and trying to juggle three hazelnuts.

"How long will it last, do you think?" Mrs Woodmouse asked.

"Ollie told me it could last seven minutes but his '*books of wisdom*', as he called them, suggested it would probably be shorter than that," Richard Robin replied.

"Where *is* Ollie Owl?" Percy Pigeon asked.

"He's probably found himself a grandstand view somewhere," Mrs Woodmouse replied.

"That certainly sounds like our Ollie," Robin said.

Mrs Woodmouse then made an interesting comment.

 "He dropped by yesterday and arranged for Woolly to deliver some nuts and an apple to him. While he was here, he told me that this was the most difficult calculation an owl had ever been called upon to resolve."

Woolly Woodmouse stopped trying to juggle and said, "It's very strange."
All eyes turned towards him.
"I tried to deliver his order a short while ago…you know… before the solar eclipse might have made it impossible. I climbed the ladder to his door and knocked but there was no reply."
"That's strange," Dotty Dormouse observed.
"There was a note pinned to his door," Woolly continued. *'No deliveries today! No visitors! Please go away! I'm not at home!'*
"That ***does*** suggest he was out," Percy said.

"He'll be back soon. No doubt he's found himself somewhere comfortable that offers a grandstand view of events as they unfold. Later he'll tell us how wise he was and that he's going to write a book about it."

'You never know with Ollie what his true intentions are,
He says he's seen the world although he never travels far.
His words are full of wisdom as he tells us every day,
But question something ludicrous…he quickly flies away!'

"…but not as quickly as *I* could fly away, of course!" Percy added.

"Have I ever mentioned that I'm a former British 300 Champion?"

There was a collective groan.

"Only three times," Robin said. "Today, that is."

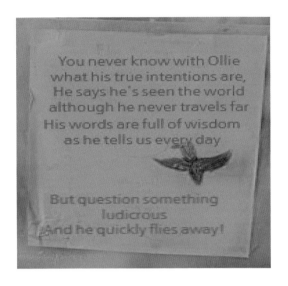

You never know with Ollie
what his true intentions are,
He says he's seen the world
although he never travels far
His words are full of wisdom
as he tells us every day

But question something
ludicrous
And he quickly flies away!

*

Ollie Owl sat at his desk and looked at the calculation again.

ΔT=62.29+0.32217.

He **should** *have written ΔT=62.92+0.32217* which clearly indicated that a solar eclipse **was** going to occur.

However, to be fair to himself, *ΔT=62.29+0.32217* **also** indicated that a solar eclipse **would** occur.

Ollie held his head between his wings and groaned softly to himself. Then he groaned a little louder. The unfortunate consequence of using $\Delta T=62.29$ instead of using $\Delta T=62.92$ meant that the solar eclipse about which he had warned and prepared the inhabitants of Undermead… was not actually going to happen *today*.

It was going to happen in one hundred years' time!

*

There was a growing volume of noisy chatter beneath the Old Oak Tree as the inhabitants of Undermead congregated in small groups.

Some groups were made up of quite angry folk and other groups were made up of those who were simply curious.

Some were simply thankful to be in the company of others and have an opportunity to voice their concerns. One of them was Dotty Dormouse.

 "I'd polished my brass candlestick and was hiding under the table with a cup of tea," she told anyone who would listen.

"I was shivering and shaking with fear and my eyes were shut tightly."

"You poor dear," said Mrs Woodmouse in a kindly tone. "How long did you stay like that?"

"Until the cuckoo in my cuckoo clock told me it was four o'clock," Dotty replied, "which meant that the phenomenon would have gone away. How can it have gone away if it never *came*? I'm sure it must be hiding somewhere waiting to pounce upon me!"

Mrs Woodhouse put an arm around her friend.

"It isn't waiting anywhere, my dear. Ollie simply made a mistake. He got it wrong."

Dotty Dormouse heaved an enormous sigh.

"It's so confusing. I don't know whether to be angry or relieved."

*

Ebenezer Eagle, Percy Pigeon and Richard Robin stood together at the bottom of the ladder that rose to Ollie Owl's front door. They were discussing what would be their wisest course of action.

"I could knock gently on the door and ask if he's feeling unwell," Robin suggested.

"*I'd* knock very loudly," Percy retorted, "and I'd ask him to show himself and explain how the wisest owl in the whole world could be so *stupid.*"

Ebenezer looked thoughtful.

"It might be best if *I* talk to him," he said. "We've known each other a long time and often pass an evening together chatting over a drink at *The Crooked Beak Variety Club.*"

*

Ebenezer Eagle ascended the ladder and tapped on

the door.

"Ollie. It's Ebenezer. Can you hear me?"

There was no reply so he knocked again.

"I know you're in there because there's the aroma of *Extra-Strong Owls-Brew Beer* creeping out from beneath your door. In fact, I wondered if we might share a bottle."

"No! I can't hear you. I'm not here," came the strained reply from within.

Ebenezer turned and peered down at the large crowd that had gathered. It was growing noisier with each passing cuckoo-tick.

He turned towards them and raised a talon to his beak. There was an immediate hush. Most folk thought it a good idea not to argue with Ebenezer.

"Nobody has said anything, Ollie. No need to feel embarrassed. There's only me here. May I come in?"

Ebenezer heard the sound of a chair scraping

across the floor. A few moments later, the door opened and a sad, rather pathetic-looking owl muttered "*Come in*."

*

The inhabitants of Undermead waited patiently.

The afternoon sun smiled brightly upon them from a cloudless azure sky.

Mrs Woodmouse had prepared a bucket of strawberry juice and Woolly Woodmouse carried it from person to person giving each a lettuce-leaf cup and a disposable reed straw.

Without warning, the door to Ollie Owl's house opened and Ebenezer Eagle stepped out.

He wrapped his talons around the top rung of the ladder and descended cautiously to the ground.

Silence also descended cautiously amongst the gathering.

Ebenezer turned to face them.

"Ollie Owl is going to address you," he informed them.

"*Address me*?" quipped Percy Pigeon. "I hope he doesn't intend to put a stamp on my wing and post me to Lower Uppermead!"

*

Ollie Owl stood on the long branch that stretched from the Old Oak Tree and adjusted his spectacles. He peered down. Everybody else peered up.

"Citizens of Undermead," he began. "I understand your frustration."

He waited for the whispering to stop.

"I...*together with others*," he added hastily, "directed you all on a journey into darkness. My...*our* intention was to prepare you for a phenomenon the like of which none of us had ever witnessed."

"We *still* haven't witnessed it. Why is that?" asked Bad Boy Badger sarcastically. He was supported by noisy cheering from his Snooty Ooty Gang.

"What you have *not* witnessed today is a solar eclipse," Ollie said.

He then looked thoughtful and added, "Who is to blame, you might well ask. *Who indeed?*"

"Er…you?" suggested a voice from the back of the crowd.

Ollie Owl took a deep breath. This was it then…

*

"You might well think that I misled you," he began.

"You might well think that it was *unwise* of me to rely on the wisdom of *others*."

"Wha'd yer mean?" Wild Boy Weasel demanded. Others nodded their heads, waggled their ears and twitched their tails in support of the question.

"***Jules Janssen!*** Blame him if you are to blame anyone!"

There was an abrupt silence.

"If Jules Janssen hadn't been present during a solar eclipse none of you would have

 suffered the indignity of having to leave your homes and meet up in a forest at midnight."

The abrupt silence continued.

"***Edmund Halley!*** You can blame him, too! It was his formula upon which I based my own extremely complicated calculations."

"However, I was browsing through '*The What, Where, When, Why, and How Guide to Watching Solar and Lunar Eclipses*' as a little light reading before addressing you…***and I discovered a printing error regarding the letter 'T' in one of*** *the formulaic equation!"*

"I realise I should have spotted the printing error sooner but I relied upon the accuracy of the printed page. My prediction regarding the arrival of a solar eclipse was, in fact, *correct*. However, the incorrectly-printed formula upon which I based my calculations means that it is not due *for another hundred years*!"

The long silence that followed was broken when Deirdre Duck from the pond at The Big House quacked,

"I can't stay beneath water that long. I've jobs to be getting on with!"

*

The inhabitants of Undermead began to drift away and return to their homes.
Most of them accepted Ollie Owl's explanation and for many his reputation for outstanding

wisdom was enhanced. The incredibly complex calculations he had generated in order to arrive at an incorrect conclusion… a conclusion brought about by ***the book publisher's printing error***…only served to enhance Ollie Owl's genius in discovering their error.

There were those who felt differently, though. "I don't believe a word of what he said," SwaggerWagger remarked as he sat outside his Summer House with Curly Cat.

"It sounded pretty convincing to me," Curly Cat replied.

"That's because you're not aristocratic Japanese Chin Dog. You didn't receive a blue-blooded education."

"I didn't receive *any* education," Curly Cat said.

"That's perfectly obvious," SwaggerWagger retorted.

"Fortunately, nobody suspects that you did."

*

Percy Pigeon was smirking but he stopped as soon as he noticed the disapproving look given him by Richard Robin.

"Okay…but *really*! Do you believe all that guff he gave us about a printing error?"

"Ollie is a close friend and friends accept other friends at face value," Richard replied.

"Well, I wouldn't value his face too highly on this occasion," Percy giggled.

Richard secretly agreed with him.

"The letter 't' indeed!" Percy continued.

"Let's forget about the *letter* 't' and think more

123

about a *cup* of tea," Richard Robin suggested.

Percy Pigeon sprang to his feet, took a short run, flapped his wings and rose into the space above his head. He tried performing a somersault in mid-air, failed, and landed on his head.

"Good idea!" he said.

*

The sun was sinking below the horizon as Ollie Owl and Richard Robin sat on the long branch of the Old Oak Tree.

"I enjoy our evening chats before heading off home to bed," Richard said.

"My evening's just beginning, of course," Ollie replied.

The branch suddenly bounced wildly. Percy Pigeon landed heavily and swayed to and fro as he tried to regain his balance.

"You should fix a couple of handles to this branch.

A pigeon could have a nasty accident."

"Wishful thinking," Ollie muttered.

*"**Coming in to land!**"*

All three looked up and were surprised to see
Ebenezer Eagle gliding towards them. He touched
down smoothly beside Percy and untied a small
package that had been attached to his left foot.

"Have you brought your own supper?" Ollie Owl
asked. "I thought we'd agreed to eat at *The
Crooked Beak Variety Club* tonight."

"We still are. This is a present for you."

"It's not my birthday," Ollie said. "Not that it
really makes a difference. I never get presents
anyway."

Percy's eyes lit up.

*"That's very sad but don't feel bad, I don't get
them either*

Even though, in racing terms, I am a high

achiever.

A medal round my neck is proof enough I am a
winner,

So open up the parcel then go off and have your
dinner!"

"Thank you, Percy. Your advice is as helpful as
ever," Ollie Owl said.

He then frowned.

"This is stranger than fiction," he mused.

Ollie took the present from Ebenezer Eagle and
began to remove the wrapping leaves.

"From whom, too-wit-too-who, is this from?" he
asked.

"The inhabitants of Undermead met up earlier this
evening and unanimously voted to thank you for
your all hard work," Ebenezer explained.

"Hard work? **What** hard work."

"Well, you studied your academic books, did many
complicated calculations and thought you had

discovered something that might cause fear and alarm amongst us."

"That's true enough," Ollie agreed. "Based on incorrect information, as I later discovered."

"But you didn't know that at the time," Ebenezer continued.

"You then thought up a very wise plan to help us prepare for the...er...phenomenon."

"True enough. True enough." Ollie said.

"I've got away with it," he thought to himself.
"They really believed me."

"And to express their gratitude they had a collection and raised sufficient fruit and nuts to buy you this present."

The last wrapping leaf fell away and Ollie looked down at the gift.

It was a book.

'Observation of the Sun and its importance in the Calculation of Time – a guide for Wise Owls.
(Revised Edition).'

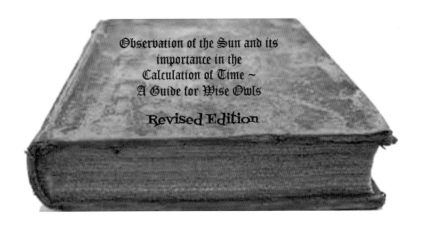

Observation of the Sun and its
importance in the
Calculation of Time ~
A Guide for Wise Owls

Revised Edition

Ollie Owl was puzzled. He scratched his head,
polished his spectacles and looked at the title
again.

Someone had scribbled the words '*Revised
Edition*' after the title!

Ollie considered his response carefully.

"This is a very thoughtful gift," he said, "and one
that will increase the fund of knowledge available
to me on those occasions when my own acuity
is…er…resting."

"***When his acuity is resting?*** What's he talking
about?" Percy Pigeon whispered to Richard Robin.

Richard smiled and answered Percy's question.
"Have you heard the expression '*to wriggle out of a difficult situation*'?" Richard said with a wink. "Well, he's wriggling!"

*

"I would like to express my gratitude to my citizens in Undermead," Ollie began …
"*His citizens*? When they we become *his citizens*?" Percy retorted.
"Shush! He'll hear you" Richard Robin warned.
Percy grinned.
"…and, no doubt, any moment now his eyes will start to revolve…"
Ollie Owl *had very good hearing* when he deemed it necessary!
He glanced up and his eyes began to revolve.
Twice to the right and three times to the left.
"*Quiet, please*! Inform the *inhabitants* of Undermead that I would like to speak to them by

the Old Oak Tree in one hour's time."

*

One hour later, Ollie Owl stepped out of his door and sauntered casually to the centre of the long branch of the Old Oak Tree.

The noise below him slowly abated until nothing could be heard apart from silence.

"Good afternoon, too-wit-to-you all!"

There was a motley assortment of '***good afternoons***' in various accents and languages from those surrounding the old oak tree. The inhabitants of Undermead were curious. What had Ollie Owl to say that was so important that they had been asked to return?

"I have asked you here this afternoon so that I might thank you for the generous gift presented to me earlier by Ebenezer Eagle."

"Cost me a day's nuts!" Squealler Squirrel blurted

out.

"**Shush**! I'll get you some more later," said Squeaky Squirrel crossly.

"The gift of the book was not only magnanimous of you. It was an inspirational choice."

Percy Pigeon glanced towards Richard Robin and mouthed the word '*magnanimous*'. Question mark.

"Ollie appreciates it," Richard explained.

"I think you will agree that the gift of the book …the **Revised Version**…only serves to confirm that I am, indeed, the wisest owl in the whole world."

Ollie paused for dramatic effect and, perhaps, ecstatic applause. Instead, he found it somewhat distracting to observe a number of Undermeaders yawning or fidgeting or, in the case of several ladies, applying make-up.

"I pointed out earlier that the reason the phenomenon, the *Solar Eclipse* I promised ou…the reason it did ***not*** occur was down to an error in the

 original book upon which I based my complicated calculations."

Ollie Owl paused again for effect and this time he was rewarded.

"***Bravo, Ollie!***" Dotty Dormouse shouted out and surprised herself by forgetting her anxious disposition for a moment or two.

"I am delighted to confirm that the ***revised version*** that you so kindly purchased for my library is now ***entirely free of errors***. I carefully studied pages two-hundred-and-six and two-hundred-and-seven a short time ago and the figures in the book now confirm and are in agreement with my original calculations."

Ollie Owl cast an anxious look at his audience. Was there anyone present perceptive enough to decipher what he had just said?

*

That evening, before Ollie Owl went looking for dinner and Richard Robin went looking for his bed, the two sat together by the Old Oak Tree and discussed the day's events.

"You sounded very convincing," Richard said.

"I sincerely hope so. My reputation is at stake," Ollie replied.

Richard Robin nodded.

"I'm sorry we had to spoil the cover of your book by adding the words *'revised version'*," he added.

Ollie shrugged.

"It required a very wise but, admittedly, a somewhat devious plan and…but *only* on this particularly unfortunate occasion…*you and Ebenezer* beat me to it!" "

But who do you think suggested adding the words

'*revised edition*' to the cover?" Richard asked.

"I suppose you managed to track down the *second* wisest owl in the world and followed his advice," Ollie Owl suggested grumpily.

"You're wrong," Richard Robin said. "*It was all Percy's idea*!"

Ollie Owl was so flabbergasted it took several ticks of a cuckoo clock before he regained his power of speech.

"Percy? The most *stupid* bird in the world?"

Richard Robin began to explain.

"He admires you, you know. Oh, he wouldn't admit to it, of course, but he once told me that some of your wise plans were even wiser than *you* thought they were."

Ollie Owl fell silent so Richard Robin continued.

"He didn't believe for *one minute* your story about the book containing an error."

"One minute in *human* time," Ollie mused.

"Would you like me to calculate how many ticks of a cuckoo clock that is?"

"*No more calculations*!" Richard exclaimed. "Not today, please!"

"Very well. Please continue."

"Percy asked Ebenezer Eagle to slip into the library of your home in the Old Oak Tree while you were out last night."

"I *did* notice a set of dirty talon-prints on my clean floor," Ollie Owl remarked.

"You'd given him a spare key to your door so he let himself in to your house and went straight to your library. On a shelf marked '*Books for Owls Educated to Owlerversity Degree Level*' he found the book that you had been studying."

Ollie Owl raised his left eyebrow.

"'*An observation of the Sun and its importance in the calculation of Time – a guide for Wise Owls*'?"

"That's the one," Richard Robin replied and then continued.

Observations of the Sun and
its importance in the
Calculation of Time
~ A Guide for Wise Owls

"He took the book to Percy Pigeon and Percy added the words '*Revised Edition*' to the title in his best Pidgin English."

Ollie Owl's eyes opened wide but they didn't swivel.

"Are you telling me that the generous gift I received this afternoon was actually *my own book* from *my own* library?"

Richard Robin nodded.

"Yes…but with the two extra words added to the title."

Ollie Owl looked flabbergasted.

"But why the Charles Dickens would Percy do a thing like that?"

"So that *you* sounded *convincing* when you told the gathering that the book contained an error." Richard paused for a moment to give Ollie some thinking time and then continued…

"If *you* knew that *we* knew it was *your* error and had *nothing* to do with the book…you might have felt too embarrassed to…er…how can I put it…you might have felt less inclined to tell the whole truth."

Richard Robin paused to allow the words to sink in.

"Percy had your concern at heart. He didn't want you to lose face. He wanted everybody to continue believing that you are the wisest owl in the whole world."

Ollie Owl was about to point out that, indeed, he *was* the wisest owl in the whole world but thought it ***a very wise plan*** to remain silent on this occasion.

"Yes, well, I er…I suppose for once I ought to be grateful to Percy."

Richard Robin smiled.

"On this occasion I think you should."

"…and I shall tell him so when I next see him," Ollie Owl replied reluctantly…

…which was a lot sooner than he had expected!

"Well, what do you know, it's me again!

I couldn't get here faster.

I've come to visit Ollie Owl

A mathematics master.

No wiser teacher can there be in any of our nations

Than Ollie Owl, the master of all solar calculations."

Percy Pigeon attempted a triple somersault,

only completed two-and-a- half and landed on his head.

"Ouch! That hurt. Hello, Ollie."

"Good evening, Percy. What a charming piece of poetry! Is it your own composition?"

"The quality speaks for itself, does it not?" Percy quipped.

"Er…of course…yes, indeed."

"Anything else you'd like to say, Ollie?"

"I…er…yes...there is actually, now you come to mention it."

"It's okay, Ollie. You can relax and start breathing normally again."

"I can?"

"'Course you can. I accept your thanks and your gratitude. Furthermore, I accept them without gloating over your embarrassment and humiliation."

Ollie Owl tried really hard to stop his eyes from swivelling. He failed. They swivelled once to the right and twice to the left, his face darkened, his mouth fell open and he seemed on the point of exploding with indignation.

Richard Robin gave him a warning look so Ollie held his composure and simply said,

"Thank you very much, Percy. I am, indeed, most grateful to you."

*

The evening wore on and it began to grow dark.

Richard Robin fluttered his wings and yawned.

"Nearly my bedtime," he said.

Ollie Owl inclined his head.

"I'm meeting Ebenezer Eagle at the *Crooked Beak Variety Club* for a glass or two of Old Tawny Owl Ale."

"Interesting," Robin remarked.

"Indeed! The whole day has been…as you say… interesting," Ollie replied. "One can learn a great deal about human kindness on an interesting day."

Richard Robin cocked his head to one side.

"If one is wise enough to look and to learn," he added.

Ollie Owl nodded sagely.

"Fortunately, that's no problem for me. When it comes down to it, when it gets to the nitty-gritty and we look at the basic fundamental nuts and bolts and basic essentials… Undermead knows I'm the wisest owl in the whole wide world."

"Or the most devious," Richard muttered as Ollie flew off for his rendezvous with Ebenezer.

THE END

(until next time)

Meet all the Whiskers, Wings and Bushy Tails characters (and the boys from The Big House) together with The Scarecrow, Farmer Giles, Rocky Ram and The Sheepish Singing Sisters (as well as others) within other books in this series. There are about twenty stories at the time of this publication of (May 2020).

Large print, colour and double-line spacing are featured.

In the early stories hyphenation is included to help pronounce some words.

Visit Amazon's Terence Braverman Page
terry@terrybraverman.co.uk
www.noteablemusic.co.uk

Printed in Poland
by Amazon Fulfillment
Poland Sp. z o.o., Wrocław

57097988R00084